Disney

Phineas and Ferb

Illustrated by Art Mawhinney

Published by Louis Weber, C.E.O., Publications International, Ltd.
7373 North Cicero Avenue, Lincolnwood, Illinois 60712

Ground Floor, 59 Gloucester Place, London W1U 8JJ

Customer Service: 1-800-595-8484 or customer_service@pilbooks.com

www.pilbooks.com

p i kids is a trademark of Publications International, Ltd., and is registered in the United States.
Look and Find is a trademark of Publications International, Ltd.,
and is registered in the United States and Canada.

8 7 6 5 4 3 2 1

Manufactured in USA.

ISBN-10: 1-4508-1103-5
ISBN-13: 978-1-4508-1103-3

pi kids ® publications international, ltd.

Phineas and Ferb have created their own backyard beach! Round up all these beach buddies before their elaborate oceanside party gets sucked into the center of the earth.

Phineas and the Ferb-Tones are on tour for one day only! Get to the Googolplex Mall so you can rock with this one-hit wonder. Find these instruments and join the band.

To satisfy their need for speed, Phineas and Ferb race their souped-up family ride at the motor speedway. Check out these things hanging around the racetrack.

Does Phineas know romance or what? *What?* Find these people on the deck of Phineas and Ferb's love boat.

Behold the watermelon of shame! Phineas and Ferb are Baljeet's only hope to win the biggest watermelon contest at the Midsummer's Festival. Can you find these folks at the festival?

Isabella's hiccups are no match for the scare tactics of Phineas and Ferb! Even scarier than what you get if you cross a yak and a Martian. Find these frightening things in the haunted house.

Phineas and Ferb's animal translator invention is helping the animals in Danville tell it like it is. Can you find these animals ready to air their grievances?

Phineas and Ferb have created the world's first truly immersive video game experience! Get sucked into the game to see if you can find these things that require jumping and ducking.

Perry the Platypus has foiled Dr. Doofenshmirtz's evil plan to destroy lawn gnomes everywhere! Go back to the beach to see if you can find 6 gnomes that were saved from certain doom.

Phineas and Ferb aren't the only one-hit wonders in their family. Their mom was Lindana, a 1980s pop star! Can you find these Lindana fans at the mall?

The Fireside Girls run a mean pit crew — go back to the racetrack to see how it's done.

Isabella is an awesome cruise director! Everyone is having fun participating in the activities she's planned. Go back to the love boat to find passengers doing these things.

- ❏ Playing shuffleboard
- ❏ Wave-pool surfing
- ❏ Playing checkers
- ❏ Ballroom dancing
- ❏ Karaoke contest
- ❏ Rock-wall climbing

Candace could end up living amongst the carnies if Ferb can't help her shrink back to normal. Go back to the Midsummer's Festival to see if you can find these people who could be Candace's future carnie BFFs.

3

Go back to the haunted house to find these frightful costumes.

If the hamster doesn't have the wheel in his cage oiled soon, he's going to lose it. Look through the Flynn-Fletcher family yard to see if you can find a few more of these pet peeves.

- ☐ A squirrel trying to open a can of nuts
- ☐ A vacuum cleaner annoying a dog
- ☐ A hamster ball stuck in a corner
- ☐ A catnap cut short
- ☐ A frog getting kissed
- ☐ A Chihuahua on TV

Who really ended up gaming the system in Phineas and Ferb's virtual video experience? Add up the points on each level to see who came out on top.

33

27

43

36

Hey! Where's Perry?

Return to each scene and find the master of disguise, Agent P.